This edition first published in 2013 by Gecko Press
PO Box 9335, Marion Square, Wellington 6141, New Zealand
info@geckopress.com

Distributed in New Zealand by Random House NZ
Distributed in Australia by Scholastic Australia
Distributed in the United Kingdom by Bounce Sales & Marketing

First American edition published in 2014 by Gecko Press USA,
an imprint of Gecko Press Ltd.
Distributed in the United States and Canada by
Lerner Publishing Group, Inc.
241 First Avenue North
Minneapolis, MN 55401 USA
www.lernerbooks.com
A catalog record for this book is available from the US Library of Congress.

A catalogue record for this book is available from the National Library of New Zealand.

creative *nz*
ARTS COUNCIL OF NEW ZEALAND TOI AOTEAROA
Gecko Press acknowledges the generous support of Creative New Zealand

Designed by Luke & Vida Kelly, New Zealand
Printed in China by Everbest Printing Co Ltd, an accredited ISO 14001 & FSC certified printer
ISBN hardback: 978-1-877467-53-0
ISBN paperback: 978-1-877467-54-7

For more curiously good books, visit www.geckopress.com

Juliette
MacIver
and
Sarah
Davis

TOUCANcan!

GECKO PRESS

For my lovely sister Vanessa,
the best of aunts, who sure can dance!
J.M.

To Sylvie and Robin, because I wish we could
come and dance with you all in Kaikoura.
S.D.

Toucan can do lots of things!

Toucan dances!
Toucan sings!

Toucan bangs a frying pan!

Can **YOU** do
what Toucan can?

Toucan can do lots of things!

Toucan slides!

Toucan swings!

Toucan hides behind a fan.
Can YOU do what Toucan can?

See him do
the cancan too.
Can you do the cancan too?

Look! Now Toucan
has a NEW plan.
With the fry pan
and a stew pan,
he can juggle
one-hand, two-hand
while he cancans
on a fruit-can!

Who can DO that?
Very few can.
Surely though, most surely,
YOU can?

BUT!

Can Toucan do
what **YOU** can do?

You can stomp and romp and hop.
You can go and you can stop.

See Toucan stomp and romp and hop ...

And skip –

and trip –

and *flip* —

and FLOP.

Poor Toucan!
What YOU can do, Toucan can
NOT.

But who can do
what kangaroo can?

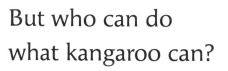

She can do
KUNG FU
with Toucan!

Can **YOU** do what kangaroo can?
Can **YOU** do kung fu with Toucan?

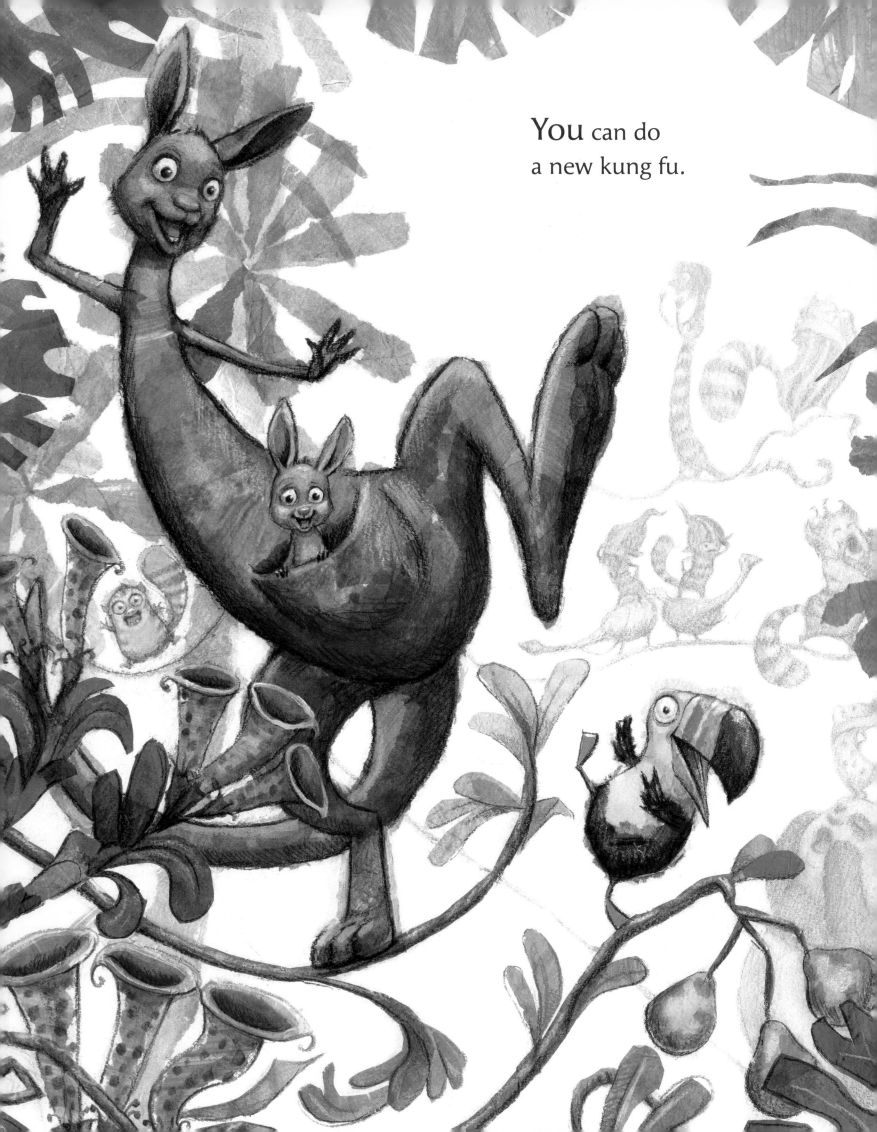

You can do
a new kung fu.

If Toucan can, can kangaroo?

Toucan has a friend or two.
One is Ewan.

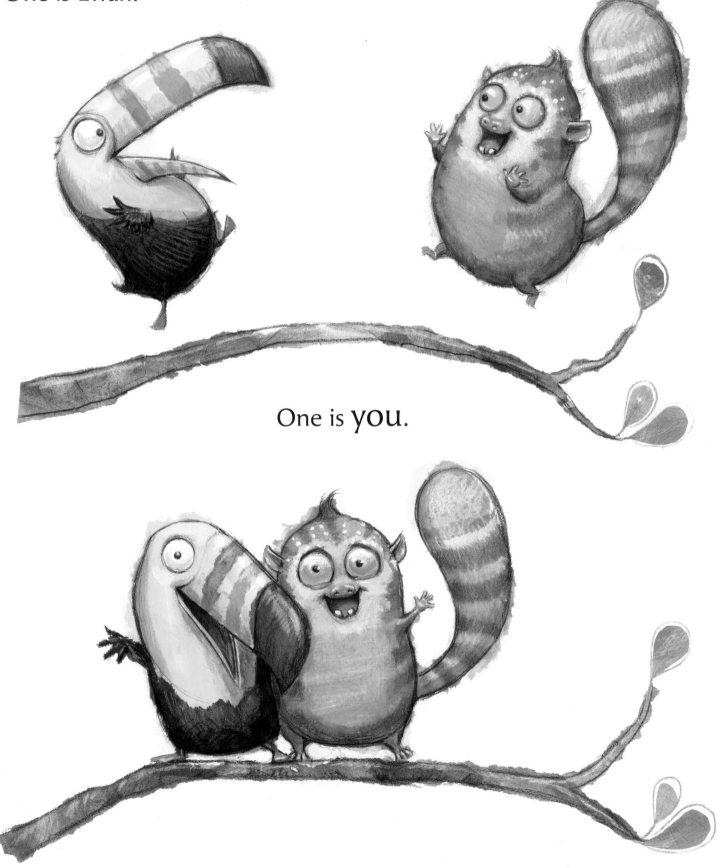

One is **you**.

Ewan loves to dance all day!
Toucan lets him lead the way.

And **YOU** can dance!
And kangaroo can!

You and Ewan dance with Toucan!

Yes, **YOU** can dance!

But Ewan's aunts
cannot
cannot
CANNOT dance.

Aunty Shanti can't at all.
And Aunty Tanya's
much too tall.

But ...

Aunty Anne and Candy can!
And Aunty Candy's panda can,

with Aunt Amanda's salamander,
Sandy's goose and Andy's gander!
And Aunt Samantha's panthers can!

When THEY all dance with Toucan, who can?
Who can dance with Toucan?

YOU can!